GW00601719

# CHANGING FACES

# CHANGING

# FACES

## A DECADE AT THE ROYAL NATIONAL THEATRE

### PORTRAITS BY JAMES F. HUNKIN
### FOREWORD BY RICHARD EYRE

TEXT EDITED BY JANET PROWTING

**OBERON BOOKS**

First published in 1997 by Oberon Books Limited
521 Caledonian Road London N7 9RH
Tel: 0171 607 3637  Fax: 0171 607 3629

Published in association with the Royal National Theatre

ISBN 1 870259 77 7

Cover and book design: Richard Doust and Andrzej Klimowski
Printed in Great Britain by BAS Printers Limited

# For Pete

## AUTHOR'S NOTE

Visiting a photographer's studio to have a portrait taken by a stranger in a strange place requires a leap of faith and in some cases a supreme act of courage. Between 1993 and 1997 I was privileged to spend time with people who revealed something of their humanity which I tried to record as honestly as I could.

I have made the final selection of 60 photographs published here, from a total collection of more than 100 to be shown at the Royal National Theatre in the summer exhibition. It is my sincere hope that I will be forgiven by those people not included.

If these photographs are nothing else, I hope they are at least a record of a group of people working together at a particular time in a particular place.

Sisu.

James Hunkin

# FOREWORD

20 may 85

Dear Richard,
Rumour has it that you are to take
over from someone called Peter Hill
at the National Theatre.

## DO NOT DO IT !

You are a ^créative ^artiste and
must not become a boring civil servant.
All artistes who get anywhere are
in danger of getting SUCKED OFF
into Administration.

IT IS **DEATH**

Yours
"Very Concerned"
Tunbridge Wells.

In 1985 I received this letter from the cartoonist Raymond Briggs. My eye was drawn to words written above a large skull and crossbones.

Sometimes, years ago now, I used to marvel at his prescience and wish that I'd heeded his advice. To remember that there was a time when I felt that making a success of running the National Theatre was as improbable as scaling the North Face of the Eiger I have to look at my diary. I write it partly for myself, and partly for an audience which I've never troubled to define: to say 'posterity' would be pompous and to say 'for publication' would be (until now) untrue. I've often been asked if, like my predecessor, I would publish my diaries and I've responded shirtily, and perhaps sanctimoniously, that I couldn't break faith with the people who have worked with me and trusted me, that I couldn't face the small betrayals of faith – the revelations of indiscretions, of insincerity, of half-truths and expedient flattery. But here is an entry from the day that it was announced that I would become Director:

> "17th January 1987. Yesterday I became Director Designate of the NT. A bizarre
> sensation. I felt very sick after the press conference, where I'd felt as if I was
> performing a character called 'Richard Eyre' – about whom I didn't have enough
> information to give a credible performance. At first I put sickness down to nerves, but
> I got home and was violently, painfully sick. Is this a metaphor for my life to be? Is
> this a sign? Caught the train this morning to Leicester v. early. Photos in most of the
> papers of this elusive 'Richard Eyre' character. I hardly recognised him. I feel no
> stirrings of epic purpose, no sense of destiny, and my ribs still ache from being sick."

A year later I am attending my first Board Meeting:

> "11th January 1988. The spectre of the *Royal* National Theatre walks abroad. Max
> clearly wants it desperately – 'an accolade' for the theatre. Bit like Judith Hart
> accepting a Damehood on behalf of the Third World. Max thinks that the NT's
> image would be enhanced. I disagree and say so. It's a useful distinction from the
> RSC, and the demotic 'NT' is attractive. To allow it to be assimilated within the orbit
> of the monarchy is to add another rivet to the theocratic state of Britain whose
> religion is the monarchy. Victor Mishcon supports Max. 'We walk in troublous seas,'
> he says. Oh England! Most of the Board seem to support me."

A few days later:

> "Wearying week at the NT. Spirits rising and falling from hour to hour. I see the
> possibility of making administrative sense of the building but not artistic sense. What
> can I **do**? What plays? And how to do them? How to make **meaning** of the work.
> That's why I'm finding it so hard to decide which plays to do. The choice is bound to
> be construed as my colours nailed to the mast."

"20th January 1988. Talk to David H. about the programme. We agreed that the problem was to define what the approach was to the classics – i.e. what is our voice? PH's voice was utterly clear text, morally neutral, visually uninflected. Ours must be more inclined to spectacle and 'interpretation', but maintaining a responsibility to the text. And I need to introduce a note of anarchy to the theatre. But there isn't an anarchistic gesture now that can't be immediately assimilated. The climate is dark and savage, and we should respond to that, not engage in the chummy humour of the times: them grinning at us grinning at them."

After several months as *de facto* Director I became official in September:

"1st September 1988. A week of almost absurd misery and insecurity. All the symptoms of nervous breakdown – tears, tiredness, lassitude, alienation, mixed with tension, self-doubt and remorse. Extreme fear mixed with total indifference."

A week later:

"Worst week yet. There are only four decisions worth making:
1. What play?
2. Who will direct it?
3. Who should be in it?
4. Who should design it?
In that order. And then the question: will anyone come and see it? To ignore that is to court disaster. I despair about bad faith, ad hoccery, being too eclectic (or having to be), and my own abilities. Am I a good enough director, am I big enough to do this job?"

It got worse. And then it got better.

It got better because I became able to trust myself, and in doing so I began to trust the people I was working with. I began to see the point of the place: that the whole could be greater than the sum of its parts. I began to see that the National Theatre worked for reasons that I was too ready to dismiss as sentimental: a sense of community, a sense of common purpose, a sense of 'family', and I began to see this not as a burden but as a strength. I began to realise that to work in the company of people for whom you feel admiration and affection at something that you feel is worth doing, for the benefit of people who share your point of view, is just about as good as life gets.

Of course, for some of the time it's been awful but, as Ingmar Bergman wrote of running the National Theatre of Sweden, it's also been "fun in an insane way, both awful and fun." It's no exaggeration, even allowing for the endemic hyperbole of the world of theatre, to say it's been the time of my life.

In the years to come I won't be lured into nostalgia: it's one of the benefits of a mildly unhappy childhood that the present tense will always seem more attractive to me than the past. This undoubtedly has a lot to do with my attraction to a medium which melts away in performance, leaving only a pile of old programmes and – if you're lucky – some precious ore glinting in the memory, while the fiascos, the failures, and the misjudgements are washed away like silt.

In the theatre, contrary to popular caricature, we're unsentimental: it's a professional necessity. When the run of a production ends, the actors leave, the posters are torn down, the sets are discarded, the furniture and costumes are consigned to the store, and a new show makes its demands on your attention, on your loyalty, on your affections. It can be unnerving to an outsider – to a civilian, as some actors would say – the ease with which we open our arms to the new troops while the veterans shunt out of the station on the other platform. Now I'm on the departing train and the theatre will carry on unsentimentally (and successfully) without me, and although I won't deny the dark and often fearful territory that I've sometimes navigated in the past ten years, I will remember only the sunlit uplands. But I won't ache to revisit them.

In 1996 I directed *John Gabriel Borkman* with a cast which included Paul Scofield, Vanessa Redgrave and Eileen Atkins. Expediently, we decided to have their faces on the poster. In spite of (or perhaps because of) a lifetime of public exposure, most actors dislike having their photograph taken quite as much as aboriginals whose lives have remained innocent of the intrusion of the twentieth century. To convince the actors that they wouldn't be mocked by the cruelty of a self-regarding opportunist I showed them a few of James Hunkin's pictures. "Mmmm," murmured Eileen with undisguised surprise, "He really likes people." It's his humanity which makes him, in my view, such an ideal chronicler of the one medium which always asserts the scale and frailty of the human face and figure.

My only regret about this book is that it's too small: to have included the faces of all those at the National Theatre who have marked my memory, earned my gratitude and won my admiration and affection, the book would be as large and heavy as a tombstone. "Policy is who you work with," said George Devine, and if theatre historians want to discover the aesthetic philosophy of my years at the National Theatre they should look no further than these pages. They will also discover who my friends were.


Richard Eyre

"Policy is who you work with."

George Devine


**Richard Eyre**

Richard is the most generous person I know,
he is one of the rare people who shows the
same genuine interest for what theatre is
becoming as for its origins and
contemporary form.


Robert Lepage

The National gave me the love of my life.

Anastasia Hille

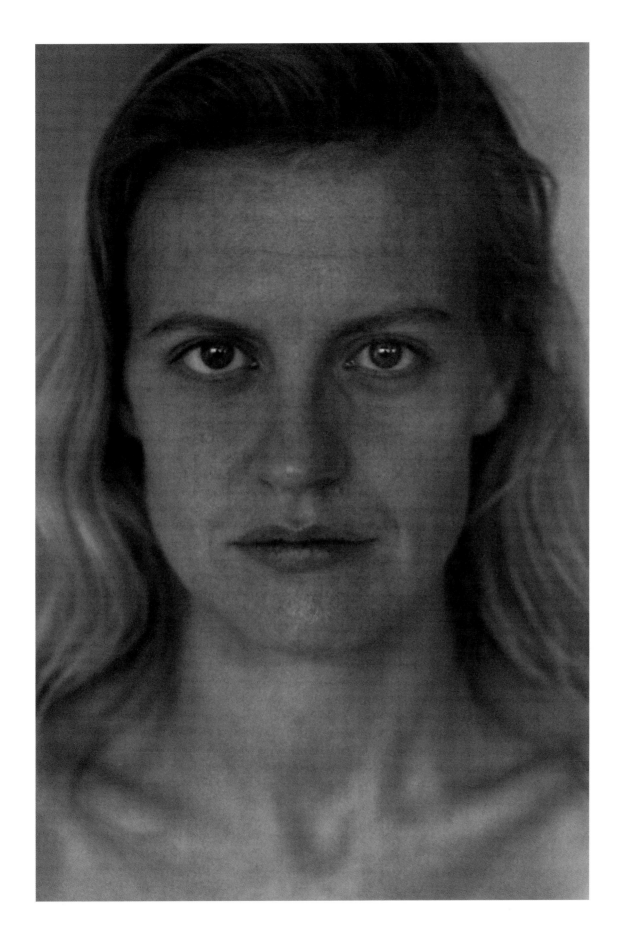

Can the same person
be tough and tender?
Can gentleness, warmth
and an open mind
go together with the
ruthless clarity that
a big organisation demands?
Can *Richard II* find the
strength of a ruler, while
avoiding the paranoia of
*Richard III*?
Yes.  Another Richard,
Richard Eyre.


Peter Brook

I was in the wilderness.
Richard rang me up.
He said "What about a new
play and a classic – *Volpone*
and *Skylight*?"
I said "Oh yeah, all right."
He's a good bloke.


Michael Gambon

Actors are often asked which of their shows are personal favourites; the ones they are most proud of. Three of mine – *Stanley, Uncle Vanya* and *Titus Andronicus* – occur during Richard's time at the National, each nurtured by him with great care. Quite apart from his other achievements, I'll always be grateful to him for those three shows.

Antony Sher

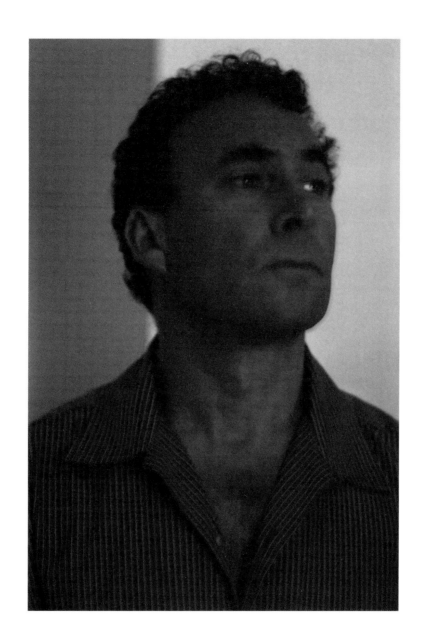

"There are many ways in which to perceive the job of play director, but I see it as being akin to that of the conductor of an orchestra."

Richard Eyre during rehearsals for *John Gabriel Borkman*

Paul Scofield

[untitled]

You'd so brilliantly directed what I wrote
with our anti-royal ranter centre-stage
that I re-read *The Prince's Play* to find a quote
to gloss my mugshot on the facing page,
but, reluctantly, decided in the end
that the lines that I liked most weren't any use –

How could I shower my newly knighted friend
with all that deeply felt republican abuse?

Tony Harrison

When I was 16 I used to wander round the building desperate to be part of it. Now I am 32, working here means the world to me.

Patrick Marber

I jus' wanna say an 'umble ta. For all the fun.

Ken Campbell

Six happy years in dix lit dep helping sked
legit top tix to boffo B.O. tuners. Variety is
the spice of life.

Giles Croft

On a Monday afternoon, after a weekend battering by the critics, Richard came to talk to the actors – a sort of 'Don't let the bastards get you down' rallying cry. He spoke with great humility and grace and the Company scampered to their dressing rooms faith somewhat restored. When things went wrong you didn't feel dumped.

Phyllida Lloyd

Learn them to dance...
And imitate the stars celestial;
For when pale death your vital twist shall sever,
Your better parts must dance with them forever.

From *Orchestra* by Sir John Davies

Jane Gibson

## Fanfare for an uncommon man

Dominic Muldowney

New joy wait on you!

From *Pericles* by William Shakespeare

**Declan Donnellan**

A good play needs no epilogue.

From *As You Like It* by William Shakespeare

**Nick Ormerod**

I had this feeling that whatever I did,
whatever choices I made, or performance I
gave, that it was as important for Richard
personally as it was for me. He has protected
the heart and soul of the National Theatre
through a total respect for the art of acting.

Ken Stott

When the fog leaves the Company stranded
at the wrong International Airport. When
the actors howl and the director jumps up
and down squealing. When old diplomatic
scores threaten to stop the show and the
chaperone has turned to the gin bottle...
I always try to give Richard a ring.


Roger Chapman

As Michael Gambon said to me at the time,
it was a lot better than working.

Alan Ayckbourn

It was the best of times.

Stephen Daldry

I went into the rehearsal room one day to rehearse *Mountain Language* and detected something odd. I couldn't at first put my finger on it but suddenly realised that everyone was dressed in black from head to foot. "Why are you all wearing black?", I asked. Miranda Richardson, Michael Gambon, Eileen Atkins, George Harris, Tony Haygarth, Julian Wadham et al raised their mugs and said in chorus very gloomily "Happy Birthday, Harold." That was a real fun loving cast.

Wearing black, I raise my mug to Richard Eyre.


Harold Pinter

No longer in Lethean foliage caught
Begin the preparation for your death
And from the fortieth winter by that thought
Test every work of intellect or faith
And everything that your own hands have wrought,
And call those works extravagance of breath
That are not suited for such men as come
Proud, open-eyed and laughing to the tomb.

From *Vacillation* by W B Yeats


David Hare

I spent six years at the National Theatre.
I made more friends, learned more and
laughed more than I ever hope to again.

Happy days.


Genista McIntosh

Thought for life (given to me at a job
interview many years ago):
'If ever you get to think you're doing rather
well, maybe you're not comparing yourself
to the right people'.


Christopher Hogg

The National's foyer before the show says it all. Audiences about to visit the three houses, mingling together in an atmosphere charged with excitement. No other theatre in my experience can match it.

Nigel Hawthorne

The National Theatre is a very desirable,
enjoyable and above all, a classy place to
work. *Viva* Richard Eyre.

Timothy Spall

I think of Richard as the Alex Ferguson of theatre – and I can't say fairer than that!

George Fenton

New stories every day, new paradoxes, opinions.
Now come tidings of maskings, mummeries,
entertainments, trophies, triumphs, revels, sports,
plays. Then again, as in a new shifted scene, new
discoveries, expeditions, now comical then
tragical matters.

Adapted from *The Anatomy of Melancholy* by Robert Burton

**Simon Russell Beale**

The National Theatre – a triumph of
content over concrete.

John Caird

I found the love of my life in the Olivier
Stalls in 1992.

Lesley Sharp

'88   oh christ
press 4   corridor   smile   start
'97   cracked it   press G


**Tom Stoppard**

Richard invited me in 1989 to play Ophelia, he then gave me <u>three</u> Hamlets, and three more brilliant roles. I felt I grew up at the National and Richard held my hand throughout.

Stella Gonet

1982.
First job in London.
*Guys and Dolls.*
Richard Eyre.
My life began.

Imelda Staunton

I have come to appreciate through my association with Richard Eyre that a pragmatic approach to diversity may result in no less a passionate and committed support for culturally-diverse theatre; above all, that such an approach ensures a continuing dialogue between the National and independent (including Asian and Black) theatre companies.

Jatinder Verma

[...Telfer enters from the Green Room]

Telfer:     Is that you, Violet?

Mrs Telfer:   Is the reading over?

Telfer:     Almost. My part is confined to the latter 'alf of
            the second act; so being close to the Green Room
            door, I stole away.

Mrs Telfer:   It affords you no opportunity, James?

Telfer:     A mere fragment.

Mrs Telfer:   Well, but a few good speeches to a man of your
            stamp –

Telfer:     Yes, but this is so line-y, Violet; so very line-y.
            And what d'ye think the character is described as?

Mrs Telfer:   What?

Telfer:     "An old, stagey, out-of-date actor."

*They stand looking at each other for a moment, silently.*

Mrs Telfer:   Will you be able to get near it, James?

Telfer:     I daresay

Mrs Telfer:   That's all right, then.

From *Trelawny of the Wells* by Arthur Wing Pinero

**Michael Bryant**

I was lucky enough to be in at the beginning. Richard knew that I had loved his production of Brecht's *Schweyk* in Edinburgh in the seventies so I jumped at the chance when he asked me to play it at the National in 1982. Then he said "By the way would you have a go at Harry the Horse in *Guys and Dolls* as well? It might work, it might not, but you've always got Schweyk...." As it turned out I think I ended up doing six performances of *Guys and Dolls* for every one of *Schweyk* but I wouldn't have missed it for the world!

Bill Paterson

As apprenticeships go it was the finest place
to be. The National equipped me and made
me feel confident as an actor and gave me the
opportunity to develop myself a great deal.

Adrian Scarborough

New organs of perception come into being
as the result of necessity – therefore increase
your necessity so that you may increase your
perception.

Jallaludin Rumi


Vicki Mortimer

I could have gone on playing Yvonne in *Les Parents Terribles* for ever: one of my 'top ten', as were the crack stage management team who made it all the more memorable.

Sheila Gish

Arriving in the concrete fortress of the
National Theatre I couldn't have imagined
the friendly and open atmosphere I would
actually find surrounding Richard. It was
extraordinary to bump into so many
directors, designers and actors in the
canteen, or in the corridors or foyers. And
all of this was happening in the incredible
concrete fortress.

Jean Kalman

A chance to gratefully acknowledge the
support and expertise of the technical teams,
a tribute to them and to Richard that the
focus is defined by a prevailing sense of
theatre.

Mark Henderson

Three memories amongst many –

Anita Reeves and Dearbhla Molloy squabbling about the yalla mallas in *The Cripple of Inishmaan*.

Kenneth MacMillan's pas de deux in *Carousel,* and the intensity of the audience's reaction to it.

Nigel Hawthorne's return to sanity as King Lear in what would be, for the benefit of those confused by Roman numerals, *King George.*

Nicholas Hytner

We shall not cease from exploration
And the end of all our exploring
Will be to arrive where we started
And know the place for the first time.

From *Little Gidding (Four Quartets)* by T S Eliot

Katie Mitchell

There is a vitality, a life force, a quickening that is translated thru you into action and because there is only one of you in all time, this expression is unique and if you block it it will not exist through any other medium and it will be lost, the world will not have it. It is not your business to determine how good it is, nor how it compares with other expressions. It is your business to keep it yours clearly and directly – to keep the channel open. You do not have to believe in yourself or your work, you have to keep open and aware to the urges that motivate you – keep the channel open. No artist is pleased. There is no satisfaction whatsoever at anytime. There is only a queer divine dissatisfaction, a blessed unrest that keeps us marching and makes us more alive than the others.

Martha Graham to Agnes de Mille

Bob Crowley

When Richard Eyre asked me to direct *The Caucasian Chalk Circle*, I said "Only if we have no one sitting in the balcony and we put them on the back of the stage", expecting a discouraging reply. The warm enthusiasm of what he really said should have come as no surprise, given not only that this was our fourth collaboration, but also the instinctive generosity and open enthusiasm with which he has opened the National's stages to outside influences: directors, experimental theatre groups, and new writers ... and Ken Campbell.

Simon McBurney

To be surrounded by the best of everything: costumes, wigs, coaching, actors, books, music, nursing, therapy, dressers, stage managers, and to feel the collective energy in the building gather around and under you as you begin the ascent to a first night is a sensation unlike any other. And Richard Eyre presided over all this in a way that was unobtrusive and all pervasive. It was reassuring to see that rather glamorous figure quietly speeding around the building intent on what should have been the impossible mission of running a tight and happy ship while directing plays as well.

Siân Phillips

*Rutherford and Son* and *The Birthday Party*, quite different plays, but both rather severe and intensely enjoyable to be in – as was the building because of the buzz of what else was going on there and the way it was being run.

Bob Peck

Richard Eyre achieved a remarkably egalitarian National Theatre. New companies and young artists flowered in his time. And myself, I grew up as a Director at the Studio, on tour and in the Cottesloe.

Tim Supple

I asked if I should pray,
But the Brahmin said,
'Pray for nothing, say
Every night in bed,
"I have been a king,
I have been a slave
Nor is there anything,
Fool, rascal, knave,
That I have not been,
And yet upon my breast
A myriad heads have lain."'

From *Mohini Chatterjee* by W B Yeats

**Fiona Shaw**

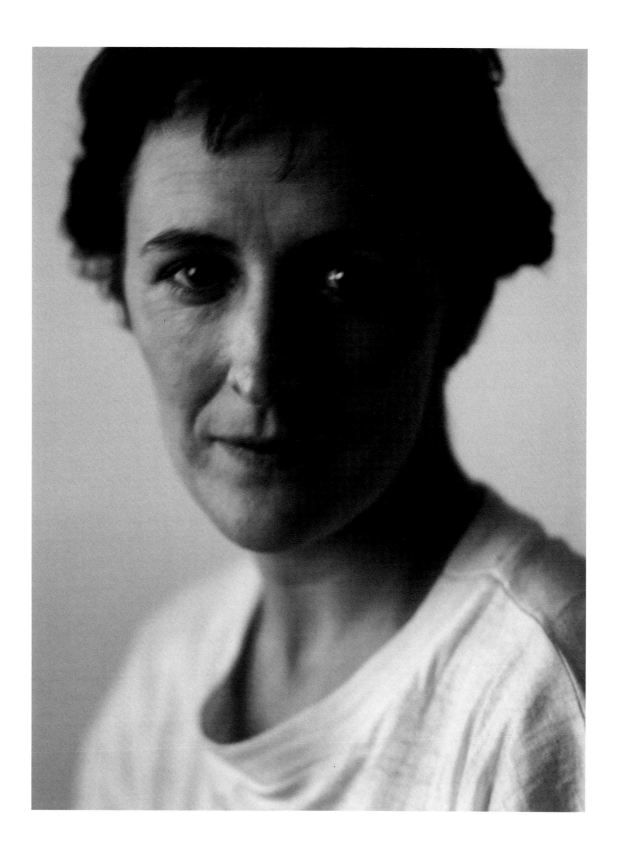

I think of Richard as a reincarnation of Harley Granville Barker – he has produced a wonderful atmosphere of reasonableness and fairness, a brilliant atmosphere to work in.

Kenneth Mackintosh

My six years with the National opened up for me a new world of enormously and variously gifted people, and exciting enterprises; and gave me the pride and satisfaction of feeling a part of a great endeavour.

Mary Soames

*Single Spies* was not without its troubles at the start, but Richard, apart from suggesting a transposition of a line to create a brilliant curtain for the second of the two plays, did nothing but exude an almost Buddhist calm about the whole thing. For a tyro director (they'd taken quite a gamble on me), this was both a lesson and an enormous relief; that things worked out as well as they did is much due to him, a man both civilised and civilising.

Simon Callow

Working at the National for a year was like coming home. I felt safe and loved and bold enough to experiment.

Frances Barber

The National has always been a great place
to mingle with the elderly.

Martin McDonagh

What tremendous memories
I'll treasure even though
The Critics panned my Sophocles
And trashed my *Cyrano*.

Ranjit Bolt

We were rehearsing *Mountain Language* and Harold (Pinter) announced that the following day was his birthday, I admire people who do that – they want the occasion marked in some way. So I suggested that we all arrive wearing black, which is a bit of a trademark with Harold. Everyone arrived duly dressed head to foot in black and when Harold came in he was casually wished a Happy Birthday. After about 30 seconds he said: "You're all looking very sombre today", and then he twigged. He seemed to enjoy it a lot. I did.

Miranda Richardson

...As a director of plays himself he must want to be in the forefront and get his hands on whatever new plays are going; as Director of the Theatre, on the other hand, he must often have to sacrifice his own ambition. I shall always be grateful to Richard that, having previously directed some of my stuff he nevertheless did not stand in the way of my working with Nicholas Hytner, particularly on *The Madness of George III*, showing a degree of magnanimity unusual in any profession let alone ours.

Alan Bennett

I will always have fond memories of the National. I have had such tremendously happy times there and hope to again – not that I'm asking for another job of course.

Judi Dench

Richard Eyre's achievement at the National stretches beyond his own lucid, inventive and passionate productions. This matchless impresario has established a true centre for British Theatre, by presenting a varied sample of regional and independent companies on the stages of the South Bank. With foreign plays in the repertoire and with visitors from across the world, his NT has also become an inter-National Theatre. Just as much as those of us he has directed and encouraged, theatre audiences are forever in his debt.

Ian McKellen

*Arcadia*. Tom Stoppard. Lyttelton 1994.
Chaos mathematics, the second law of
thermo dynamics ... well at
least I remember a couple of things about
Byron ... or do I ... ?

Trevor Nunn

RICHARD EYRE, 1993
DIRECTOR OF THE NATIONAL 1988-1997
PAGE 11

ROBERT LEPAGE, 1997
PRODUCER, DIRECTOR, ACTOR
PAGE 13

ANASTASIA HILLE, 1994
ACTOR
PAGE 15

PETER BROOK, 1994
PRODUCER, DIRECTOR
PAGE 17

MICHAEL GAMBON, 1997
ACTOR
PAGE 19

ANTONY SHER, 1996
ACTOR
PAGE 21

PAUL SCOFIELD, 1997
ACTOR
PAGE 23

TONY HARRISON, 1996
POET, DIRECTOR
PAGE 25

PATRICK MARBER, 1997
WRITER, DIRECTOR
PAGE 27

KEN CAMPBELL, 1996
WRITER, ACTOR
PAGE 29

GILES CROFT, 1996
LITERARY MANAGER 1989-1995
PAGE 31

PHYLLIDA LLOYD, 1996
DIRECTOR
PAGE 33

JANE GIBSON, 1996
DIRECTOR OF MOVEMENT
PAGE 35

DOMINIC MULDOWNEY, 1996
COMPOSER, DIRECTOR OF MUSIC
PAGE 37

DECLAN DONNELLAN, 1994
DIRECTOR, ASSOCIATE
PAGE 39

NICK ORMEROD, 1994
DESIGNER
PAGE 41

KEN STOTT, 1997
ACTOR
PAGE 43

ROGER CHAPMAN, 1997
HEAD OF TOURING
PAGE 45

ALAN AYCKBOURN, 1997
WRITER, DIRECTOR
PAGE 47

STEPHEN DALDRY, 1994
DIRECTOR
PAGE 49

HAROLD PINTER, 1994
WRITER, DIRECTOR
PAGE 51

DAVID HARE, 1993
WRITER, DIRECTOR, ASSOCIATE
PAGE 53

GENISTA MCINTOSH, 1996
EXECUTIVE DIRECTOR 1990-1996
PAGE 55

CHRISTOPHER HOGG, 1996
CHAIRMAN OF THE BOARD FROM 1995
PAGE 57

NIGEL HAWTHORNE, 1994
ACTOR
PAGE 59

TIMOTHY SPALL, 1997
ACTOR
PAGE 61

GEORGE FENTON, 1997
COMPOSER
PAGE 63

SIMON RUSSELL BEALE, 1997
ACTOR
PAGE 65

JOHN CAIRD, 1993
DIRECTOR
PAGE 67

LESLEY SHARP, 1996
ACTOR
PAGE 69

TOM STOPPARD, 1993
WRITER, BOARD MEMBER FROM 1989
PAGE 71

STELLA GONET, 1997
ACTOR
PAGE 73

IMELDA STAUNTON, 1997
ACTOR
PAGE 75

JATINDER VERMA, 1996
PRODUCER, DIRECTOR
PAGE 77

MICHAEL BRYANT, 1993
ACTOR, ASSOCIATE
PAGE 79

BILL PATERSON, 1997
ACTOR
PAGE 81

ADRIAN SCARBOROUGH, 1996
ACTOR
PAGE 83

VICKI MORTIMER, 1997
DESIGNER
PAGE 85

SHEILA GISH, 1996
ACTOR
PAGE 87

JEAN KALMAN, 1994
LIGHTING DESIGNER
PAGE 89

MARK HENDERSON, 1996
LIGHTING DESIGNER
PAGE 91

NICHOLAS HYTNER, 1993
DIRECTOR, ASSOCIATE
PAGE 93

KATIE MITCHELL, 1994
DIRECTOR
PAGE 95

BOB CROWLEY, 1993
DESIGNER, ASSOCIATE
PAGE 97

SIMON McBURNEY, 1997
PRODUCER, DIRECTOR, ACTOR, WRITER
PAGE 99

SIÂN PHILLIPS, 1996
ACTOR
PAGE 101

BOB PECK, 1997
ACTOR
PAGE 103

TIM SUPPLE, 1996
DIRECTOR
PAGE 105

FIONA SHAW, 1993
ACTOR
PAGE 107

KENNETH MACKINTOSH, 1997
STAFF DIRECTOR
PAGE 109

MARY SOAMES, 1996
CHAIRMAN OF THE BOARD 1988-1995
PAGE 111

SIMON CALLOW, 1996
ACTOR, DIRECTOR, WRITER
PAGE 113

FRANCES BARBER, 1996
ACTOR
PAGE 115

MARTIN McDONAGH, 1997
WRITER
PAGE 117

RANJIT BOLT, 1997
TRANSLATOR
PAGE 119

MIRANDA RICHARDSON, 1996
ACTOR
PAGE 121

ALAN BENNETT, 1993
WRITER, ACTOR, DIRECTOR
PAGE 123

JUDI DENCH, 1997
ACTOR
PAGE 125

IAN McKELLEN, 1997
ACTOR
PAGE 127

TREVOR NUNN, 1996
DIRECTOR DESIGNATE, 1997
PAGE 129

## ACKNOWLEDGEMENTS

I wish to thank Richard Eyre for his faith and trust in allowing me a rare opportunity to express myself freely through these portraits. For me then to find a publisher with James Hogan's vision and conviction is beyond any natural expectation of good fortune. Janet Prowting's selfless dedication to all that has come with the editing of this book, and personal support at critical moments has made this work a pleasure.

My thanks also go to all those at Oberon Books – Richard Doust, Andrzej Klimowski, Sarah Wherry, Kirstie Fry, and not least, Charles Glanville. At the National Theatre I would also like to thank Lyn Haill for her calm and kindness, and Oliver Prenn for his financial assistance in the early stages of the project.

Thanks, of course, to all the sitters for their patience, encouragement and trust, and to their personal assistants who helped to organise the sittings. I would also like to thank the Camera Club in Kennington for providing a unique facility for me to develop my craft.

Without the loyalty and love of my family and friends my efforts would have amounted to very little. My eternal thanks to Mum & Dad, and Stace – the brightest star in my heaven.

And, if you're watching up there, thanks for infinite inspiration and guidance to R. van Rijn and Mr Steichen.

## PUBLISHER'S ACKNOWLEDGEMENTS

Excerpt from *Little Gidding* from FOUR QUARTETS by T. S. Eliot reproduced in the UK by permission of Faber and Faber Ltd and in the US by Harcourt Brace & Company. Excerpts from *Vacillation* and *Mohini Chatterjee* by W. B. Yeats from THE COLLECTED WORKS OF W. B. YEATS Volume 1: THE POEMS, Revised and Edited by Richard J. Finneran, reproduced in the UK by permission of A. P. Watt Ltd on behalf of Michael Yeats and in the US by permission of Simon & Schuster. Excerpt from *Trelawny of the Wells* by Arthur Wing Pinero reprinted by permission of Samuel French Ltd on behalf of the Trustees of the estate of Arthur Wing Pinero.

*Colophon*
CHANGING FACES IS TYPESET IN
ADOBE GARAMOND & GARAMOND EXPERT
WITH BELL GOTHIC
THE PHOTOGRAPHS ARE REPRODUCED
IN DUOTONE AND PRINTED ON
PARALUX CREAM 150 GSM
1997